SNOW

For James

A TEMPLAR BOOK

First published in the UK in 2014 by Templar Publishing,
an imprint of The Templar Company Limited,
Deepdene Lodge, Deepdene Avenue, Dorking, Surrey, RH5 4AT, UK
www.templarco.co.uk

First edition

ISBN 978-1-78370-072-1 (hardback)
ISBN 978-1-78370-073-8 (paperback)

Designed by Mike Jolley
Edited by Libby Hamilton

Printed in Malaysia

Sam Usher

SNOW

templar publishing

When I woke up
this morning, it
was snowing!

I couldn't wait to
go to the park.

All I needed to do
was dress,

wash, put my
shoes on,

and get Grandad.

We had to get outside
in the snow…

… before anyone else.

I was ready to go,
but Grandad wasn't.

I said, "Don't forget
the snow!"

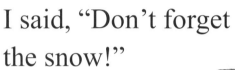

And he said,
"Don't forget your scarf."

So we weren't quick enough to be first.

Grandad was taking ages.
So I shouted,

"All the others will
get there first, Grandad –
DON'T FORGET
THE SNOW!"

And Grandad said,
"Don't forget
your hat!"

So we weren't quick enough
to go with my friends.

Grandad was taking absolutely **ages**. So I shouted,

"HURRY UP, GRANDAD!"

And he said, "It's okay, we're not going to miss the fun."

But we were! I told him **all** the cats and dogs were out there.

Grandad laughed and said the whole zoo
was probably out there.

And then I saw something…

I did!

Finally, Grandad was ready.

We were off to the park.

Where I could have fun with everyone at last.

We played all the games you can play in the snow.

Grandad won the snowball fight
by six slushings to four.

So I think he had fun too.

Back at home,
Grandad and
I agreed some
things are
definitely worth
waiting for.

I hope it snows
again tomorrow.

The End